A CLASSIC TALE

The Three Little Pigs

Illustration: Agustí Asensio
Adaptation: Eduard José

Retold by Janet McDonnell

🎈 The Child's World, Inc.

Once upon a time, there were three little pigs. When they grew old enough, the three pigs left their parents and went to live on their own. Now the three brothers were all hard workers, and they liked each other very much. So it was not surprising that they all had the same idea at once:

"What do you think . . ." said the first.

". . . about building . . ." said the second.

". . . a little house?" said the third.

"A little house for all three or three different houses?" asked the eldest. In the end, they decided to build three houses close together. That way they could be neighbors as well as brothers.

The three little pigs went right to work. The smallest of the three found a farmer who was piling straw on the edge of a cornfield.

"Could you give me a bit of this straw to build my house?" asked the little pig.

"Help yourself!" answered the farmer.

The little pig went right to work building his house of straw.

The middle pig was strolling through the woods when he came across a huge pile of branches and leaves. There were so many branches and leaves that the pig thought he would build his house with them. So he loaded them up and carried them next to the place where his little brother was building his straw house. There the middle pig began building his own house of branches.

The eldest pig, who was also the wisest, went in search of bricks and mortar. He carried them to the place next door to his brothers' houses of straw and branches and went right to work.

During the weeks which followed, the three little pigs were busy building their houses. Naturally, the first one to finish was the little pig with the house of straw. Then the one with the house of branches finished his. Last of all, the pig with the bricks and mortar finished building his house.

"How pretty they are!" The three brothers looked at them with pride.

And the three houses were really splendid, each in its own way. To finish off the work, the little pigs put up a long fence around their houses and painted it red.

The three little pigs were very happy in their new homes. They got up early to go to work. The eldest collected honey and sold it. The middle pig grew vegetables. And the youngest milked the cows for a neighboring farmer. Then, when they came home from work, the three sat in their little garden and chatted about the things they had done during the day, as they watched the sun go down.

But one morning, the peace and quiet of their lives was suddenly shattered. A fierce wolf came creeping out of the woods. Besides being quite cruel, the wolf was terribly hungry. As he passed by the houses, he sniffed the air.

"I smell tender piglet!" he said.

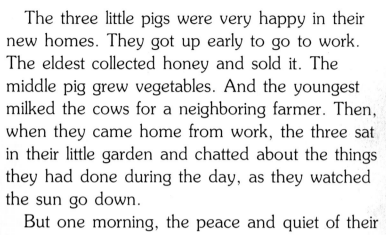

He followed the scent to the house of the littlest pig, the one with the house of straw. The hungry wolf knocked at the door.

"Who is it?" asked the little pig.

"Mr. Wolf," answered the wild beast. "I've come to bring you some medicine for your aches and pains."

But the little pig did not fall for that. He knew wolves only too well.

"Go away! Be off with you!" he said.

But the angry wolf did not go away. He filled his lungs with all the air they would hold and blew onto the straw house like a tornado. The house crumbled down in ruins. The little pig just had time to run to his brother's house of branches and lock himself inside. The wolf ran after him and knocked at the door.

"Open the door! I've brought a delicious pie which I've baked for you all."

"Be off with you!" said the little pig and the middle pig, locking and bolting the door.

But the hungry wolf did not go away. He filled his lungs with air again and huffed and puffed. It was harder for him this time, but he finally blew down the middle pig's house of branches and leaves. The two brothers escaped to the eldest pig's house.

As soon as the wolf saw the house of bricks and mortar, he knew that the building was too solid for him to be able to blow it down easily. So once again, he tried to trick the pigs. He knocked on the door and said:

"Open the door, my dear little pigs. It's the mailman, and I have a letter from your parents."

"You can't fool us," said the eldest pig. "Our parents live nearby, and we saw them only yesterday."

The evil wolf cursed the three little pigs for being so smart. Then he huffed, and he puffed, and he huffed, and he puffed, but it was no use. The house of brick stood firm and solid. But there is no one more stubborn than a hungry wolf, and so he huffed and puffed outside the door for hours and hours. When evening came, the wolf was so exhausted he couldn't stand up, and his tongue was hanging out of his mouth. But the house was still standing.

"All right," he croaked, "sooner or later you'll have to come out! And the moment you set foot outside the door, I'll be right here waiting to gobble you up."

The little pigs did not believe the wolf's threat and went to sleep. They were sure that the next morning their enemy would no longer be outside the house. But they were wrong. The wolf spent the night on the porch and never took his eyes off the door.

"We've had it!" said the littlest pig. "This animal will never give up the hunt."

"Leave it to me! Don't be afraid!" said the eldest pig firmly. And to the surprise of his brothers, he lit the fire in the fireplace and covered the chimney which let the smoke out of the house.

"The house is filling up with smoke!" said the middle pig. "Don't you think that you're making matters worse?"

The youngest pig just coughed, "Ugh, ugh," because the thick smoke was getting into his lungs. When the fire was blazing so fiercely that the flames were almost reaching the furniture, the eldest pig went to the door and shouted through it as loudly as he could.

"That wolf is a fool!" he shouted. "He doesn't know that we've got enough food here to last for months and that we have no need to go out. He'll die of hunger first! Yes, I tell you he's a fool. He doesn't know that he could catch us easily if he climbed down the chimney!"

On the other side of the door, the wolf, of course, heard these words, just as the little pig wanted him to.

"So I'm a fool, am I?" he thought to himself.

He snuck around the house and jumped up onto the roof. He tiptoed carefully over the tiles and went up to the chimney.

"I'll swallow them down in one gulp," he said to himself. He swung his legs into the chimney and began to climb down.

Inside the house, the little pigs were roasting. They couldn't take much more heat. But the eldest brother knew just what he was doing. He heard the wolf's footsteps on the roof. When he thought the beast was climbing down the chimney, he threw open the chimney chute and the flames and smoke shot up the sides. The bonfire leapt right up to the wolf. With a terrible howl, he fell into the flames and died faster than it takes to tell.

"Hurray!" shouted the three little pigs. They had beaten the wolf, and that called for a celebration. But before they could celebrate, they had business to take of—the little pig and the middle pig had nowhere to live.

"What do you think . . ." said the eldest pig.

". . . about building a house . . ." said the middle pig.

". . . three stories high?" said the littlest pig.

"That's it!" said the eldest. "And it must be built of bricks and mortar like this one. Then no wolf can blow it down!"

They set to work and built two new stories on top of the brick house that had served them so well. And so, as well as being brothers and neighbors, they could share the same elevator.

After that, no wolf ever dared to bother them again. They are still there, the eldest gathering honey and selling it, the middle one growing vegetables, and the little one milking the cows of a neighboring farmer.